Museum of Lost Things
A YA Cozy Mystery

LIA LUCAS

Museum of Lost Things
A YA Cozy Mystery
Copyright © 2025 by Lia Lucas
All rights reserved.

Book Cover and formatting provided by Trisha Fuentes
https://bit.ly/m/trishafuentes

No part of this book may be reproduced in any form or by any electronic or mechanical means, including information storage and retrieval systems, without written permission from the author, except for the use of brief quotations in a book review.

ISBN: 979-8-3485-0134-1 (Paperback)

Published by
Ardent Artist Books
www.ardentartistbooks.com

ABOUT ARDENT ARTIST BOOKS

ABOUT US

Ardent Artist Books was established in 2008

We publish modern and historical romances once a month!

Get Your FREE List: Published & Upcoming Books
visit our website at:
https://bit.ly/3Wva4o0

* * *

➥ WE HAVE BOOK TRAILERS

Follow us on YouTube!
https://bit.ly/3W3xn7a

Like, Subscribe & Comment

➥ **WE HAVE SERIALIZED FICTION!**

Visit our website today to download one of our stories that unfold in bite-sized pieces!

Each installment is just 99¢!

https://bit.ly/3LsDpJL

* * *

➥ **LET'S CONNECT!**

Fuel your love of fiction with exclusive content and captivating insights from Ardent Artist Books. Whether you crave the thrill of modern narratives or the timeless elegance of historical fiction, our newsletter delivers a curated selection straight to your inbox. Plus, as a welcome gift, receive a FREE downloadable eBook:

"The Family Fix"
https://bit.ly/49BR3UB

CONTENTS

1. The Museum — 1
2. Donations — 15
3. The Disappearance — 27
4. Investigation — 41
5. Heirlooms — 51
6. Artistic Discoveries — 61
7. Searching for Clues — 69
8. A Local Historian — 77
9. The Intruder — 85
10. Common Ground — 93
11. Gathering Info — 101
12. Hushed Tones — 111

YOU MIGHT ALSO LIKE

Journey to Crystal Lake — 129
Snowbound with the Boy Next Door — 131
Star-Crossed Rivals — 133
Haunted Hearts — 137
The Secret Recipe Society — 139
The Midnight Gardent Club — 141

About Lia — 143
Also by Lia — 145

CHAPTER 1
THE MUSEUM

Morning sunlight dances through the maple trees lining Main Street, creating shifting patterns on the sidewalk as I hurry toward my first day as an intern. My shoes click against the concrete, matching the excited rhythm of my heart. Uncle Stephen might've helped secure this position at the Museum of Oddities, but I'm determined to prove I earned it on my own merits.

The museum's brick facade rises before me, its weathered exterior sporting vibrant banners that flutter in the summer breeze.

"WHERE HISTORY MEETS MYSTERY"

I can't help but smile. As a junior who's spent more time sketching artifacts in notebooks than hanging at the mall, this feels like my moment.

I pause at the heavy wooden doors, running my fingers over the brass handle. The cool metal grounds me, reminding me this is real. I've visited dozens of times before, but today's different. Today, I'm part of the museum's story.

The door creaks open, and that familiar scent hits me – old wood, leather-bound books, and something distinctly mysterious that I've never been able to name. It wraps around me like a welcome hug, instantly calming my nerves.

"Mei! Oh my god, you're here!" Clara's voice (my BFF) rings through the foyer as she bounces toward me, her vintage-inspired dress swishing around her knees. She's paired it with chunky boots and a denim jacket covered in pins – classic Clara style. "Can you believe we actually get to work here?"

"I know! I've been up since five, too excited to sleep." I adjust my messenger bag, filled with fresh notebooks and my favorite sketching pencils. "The new exhibits look amazing."

"Wait till you see the folk art collection they just got in." Clara grabs my arm, her eyes sparkling. "We should totally check it out during lunch. I heard there's this really cool piece that-"

"Already trying to corrupt the new intern with unauthorized tours?" Drew's voice cuts in, teasing. My cousin leans against a display case containing what looks like an ancient typewriter, his shaggy brown hair falling into his eyes. He's wearing his favorite NASA t-shirt – the one that's been washed so many times the logo's starting to fade.

"Please, like you haven't already mapped out every secret corner of this place." I bump his shoulder as I pass.

"Someone's got to know where all the good hiding spots are." He grins, falling into step beside me. "Besides, who else is gonna help you slack off during inventory duty?"

"I heard that, Mr. Caldwell." A warm voice joins our conversation, and we turn to see Ms. Martinez approaching. Today she's wearing a flowing turquoise dress with a golden scarf draped artfully around her shoulders, her dark curls pulled back in a loose bun. "And I sincerely hope you're joking about slacking off."

Her eyes crinkle with amusement as she reaches us. "Welcome to your first official day at the Museum of

Oddities. I can't tell you how excited I am to have such enthusiastic young people joining our team."

"We're honored to be here, Ms. Martinez," I say, meaning every word.

"The museum isn't just about preserving artifacts," she continues, gesturing to the displays around us. "It's about keeping stories alive, connecting people to their past, and sometimes" – her eyes twinkle – "uncovering mysteries we never knew existed. Each object here has a tale to tell, and now you'll help share those stories with our community."

Looking at Drew joking around with Clara, I can't help but smile. He's been my partner-in-crime since we were kids building blanket forts during Thanksgiving and staging elaborate Easter egg hunts that would drive our parents crazy. Every family gathering, every holiday, every milestone - Drew's been there. When I struggled with math in seventh grade, he spent hours breaking down equations until they finally clicked. When he needed someone to test his wild science fair projects, I was his willing guinea pig, even after that infamous robot vacuum incident that left us both covered in glitter for days. He knows exactly when to crack a joke to lift my spirits and when to just sit quietly and let me vent.

It's like having a built-in best friend who also happens to share half your DNA.

Some people don't get how cousins can be as close as siblings, but Drew and I have always been different. Maybe it's because we're both only children, or maybe it's because our parents are so close - my mom and his dad are siblings who never lost that tight bond even after starting their own families. Whatever the reason, Drew's been more than just a cousin to me. He's the person who helped me through my awkward middle school phase, who defended me when kids made comments about my mixed heritage, who shows up with ice cream and terrible puns when I'm having a rough day. Now, standing here in the museum where we'll be working together all summer, it feels right that we're starting this new adventure as a team.

Clara bounces on her toes as Ms. Martinez hands out our orientation packets, her dark hair swishing with each movement. I catch her eye and we share our trademark look - the one we perfected in second grade when we both showed up to school wearing matching butterfly hair clips. Back then, we were just two artsy kids who bonded over our shared love of drawing during recess. Now, twelve years later, we're still finishing each other's sentences.

"This is going to be the most amazing—" Clara starts.

"Summer ever," I complete, making her grin.

"Just like that time in fourth grade when we—"

"Tried to start our own museum in your garage?" I laugh, remembering how we'd arranged all our prized possessions - my rock collection, her vintage costume jewelry from her grandmother, and about fifty stuffed animals - into careful displays. "Your mom was so patient with us taking over her parking spot."

"Until it rained and we had to bring everything inside." Clara adjusts one of the pins on her jacket - the one I gave her for her birthday last year, with a paint palette design. "Remember how we charged everyone a quarter to see our 'rare artifacts'?"

"And Drew was our only customer." I smile at my cousin, who's pretending to be absorbed in his orientation packet but I know he's listening. "He paid extra to see the 'dinosaur bone' that was actually just a weirdly shaped stick."

"Hey, that was a quality stick," Drew protests. "Worth every penny."

Clara and I have been inseparable since that first art class. Through middle school drama, high school crushes, and family ups and downs, she's been my constant. When my grandma passed away last year, Clara showed up at my door with a sketchbook full of memories we'd drawn together over the years. She sat with me for hours, adding new drawings and sharing stories until the hurt felt a little less sharp.

"You guys are going to love the art restoration room," Ms. Martinez says, leading us down a corridor. "We just got some fascinating pieces in that need careful documentation."

"Perfect for our resident artists," Drew teases, nudging me.

Clara grabs my arm excitedly. "Just like when we restored your mom's old—"

"Photo albums!" I exclaim. "That was such a disaster at first."

"Until we figured out how to—"

"Use rice paper and archival glue." I shake my head, remembering our determined twelve-year-old selves hunched over the dining room table, carefully piecing together forgotten family photos.

Ms. Martinez pauses by a heavy wooden door. "I see you

two have some experience with preservation techniques?"

"They're basically the same person in two bodies," Drew explains. "It's kind of terrifying sometimes."

"It's not terrifying," Clara and I say simultaneously, then burst out laughing.

Drew throws up his hands in mock surrender. "I rest my case."

Looking at Clara now, her face bright with excitement as she takes in the museum's artifacts, I'm struck by how much we've grown together. From the silly kids who spent hours creating elaborate stories about each item in our makeshift museum, to teenagers about to start a real internship, we've never lost that spark of shared creativity and wonder.

"This summer is going to be different though," Clara whispers as Ms. Martinez unlocks the door. "We're actually going to be working with real historical pieces, not just pretending anymore."

I squeeze her hand. "At least we had good practice with your mom's antique teacup collection."

"Which we only dropped one of—"

"And managed to fix before she noticed."

Ms. Martinez turns back to us, her scarf catching the light. "I have a feeling you two are going to bring some special energy to our little museum family."

Drew rolls his eyes good-naturedly. "You have no idea what you're in for, Ms. Martinez. These two once spent an entire weekend cataloging every single book in both their houses by genre, color, and 'mystical potential.'"

"The system worked perfectly," Clara defends.

"Still does," I add, thinking of our color-coded bookshelves at home. Some things never change, and I'm grateful for that. Having Clara by my side makes everything feel more like an adventure, even something as simple as organizing books or, now, documenting museum artifacts.

My fingers tap against the wooden desk as Ms. Martinez's orientation speech continues. The museum's layout map blurs before my eyes, and my mind wanders to the unexplored corners she mentioned earlier. Fifteen minutes have passed, but it feels like hours. Every creak of the floorboards, every shadow cast by the vintage light fixtures sparks a new possibility in my imagination.

"And remember, proper documentation is essential," Ms. Martinez gestures to the thick binder in front of us. "Every item that comes through these doors has a story, and it's our job to preserve it."

I steal a glance at Drew, who's doodling robots in the margins of his orientation packet. Clara's actually taking notes, her purple pen flying across the page. My own notebook remains pristine, waiting for the sketches and observations I'm dying to make.

The folk art collection Clara mentioned earlier calls to me like a siren song. I picture weathered wooden figures, hand-stitched quilts with hidden meanings, paintings that capture moments lost to time. My fingers itch to trace their outlines in my sketchbook, to capture their essence before they're cataloged and stored away.

"Now, for your first assignment," Uncle Stephen's voice cuts through my daydream as he enters the room. He's wearing his curator badge and his serious expression – the one that means business. "We need the donation room organized before the new exhibit installation next week."

My heart sinks a little. The donation room. Also known as the museum's catch-all space where well-meaning citizens drop off everything from great-grandma's butter churn to supposedly haunted dolls. It's probably dusty, definitely cluttered, and absolutely not what I had in mind for my first day.

"Each item needs to be photographed, logged, and properly stored," Uncle Stephen continues, handing out assignment sheets. "Pay special attention to provenance – where these items came from, who owned them, any historical significance."

Drew catches my eye and mouths "haunted dolls." I bite back a laugh, remembering our childhood theory that the donation room was actually a portal to another dimension. We'd spent countless visits pressing our faces against its frosted glass window, convinced we'd seen shadows move on their own.

"This is actually perfect," Clara whispers, nudging me. "We'll get first dibs on seeing all the new stuff."

She's right, of course. The donation room could hold anything – forgotten treasures, mysterious artifacts, pieces of local history waiting to be discovered. But right now, Uncle Stephen's given me a job to do, and I need to prove myself worthy of this internship.

"I've divided you into teams," Uncle Stephen says, checking his clipboard. "Clara and Lisa will start with textiles. Drew and James handle furniture and larger items. Mei, you'll be working with documentation and smaller artifacts."

My heart does a little jump. Documentation means handling the items directly, examining them up close, researching their stories. Maybe this assignment isn't so bad after all.

"Remember," Ms. Martinez adds, "if you find anything unusual or potentially valuable, flag it immediately. We've had some... interesting donations in the past."

The way she hesitates on "interesting" makes me wonder what kind of surprises are waiting in that room. I've heard stories about people finding priceless antiques mixed in with garage sale leftovers, or uncovering long-lost historical documents stuffed in old books.

Uncle Stephen hands me a pair of white cotton gloves and a camera. "Start with the boxes by the window. And Mei?" He pauses, his expression softening slightly. "I know how thorough you are with your sketches, but try to focus on processing items efficiently. We've got a lot to get through."

I nod, though my sketchbook weighs heavily in my bag. He knows me too well – knows I'd spend hours capturing every detail if given the chance. But he's right. This isn't about indulging my artistic impulses; it's about proving I can handle real museum work.

The donation room key feels heavy in my hand as our group moves toward the mysterious space. Sunlight filters through the frosted glass, casting strange shadows on the boxes and covered furniture inside. The door creaks open, releasing a wave of musty air and endless possibilities.

"Ready to make history?" Drew asks, bumping my shoulder as we enter.

"More like ready to organize history," I reply, but I can't keep the excitement out of my voice. Even with the dust and the daunting task ahead, I'm exactly where I want to be.

Clara immediately gravitates toward a trunk overflowing with vintage clothing. James and Drew start uncovering furniture, while Lisa sorts through a box of old photographs. I make my way to the window, where neat rows of boxes await my attention.

CHAPTER 2
DONATIONS

The morning sun streams through the museum's stained glass windows, painting rainbow patterns across the worn wooden floors. I can't help but smile as I watch Drew attempt to balance a stack of empty archival boxes while Clara documents their inventory numbers.

"Watch it, butterfingers!" I call out as one box starts to slip.

Drew catches it with his chin, his freckled face scrunching up in concentration. "I got this, I got this!"

"Sure you do." Clara snaps a quick photo of him with her phone. "This is definitely going in the intern highlights reel."

Ms. Martinez's heels click against the floor as she approaches our little group, her bright orange scarf trailing behind her like a monarch butterfly's wings. "Good morning, my eager historians! Ready to dive into something exciting?"

"Always!" I straighten up, tucking my pen behind my ear.

My heart skips a beat. This is exactly what I've been waiting for – real artifacts with real histories to uncover.

I bounce on my toes as I approach the first box, memories flooding back of countless hours spent sprawled on my bedroom floor with history books spread around me like fallen autumn leaves. The familiar musty scent of aged paper wafts up as I lift the lid, reminding me of weekends at the library where I'd lose myself in tales of ancient civilizations and forgotten treasures.

"You've got that look again," Drew says, setting down his stack of empty boxes. "The one where you're about to go full history nerd on us."

"Can't help it." I carefully lift out what appears to be an old brass compass. "Remember when we were ten and I made you help me dig up the backyard because I was convinced there were Revolutionary War artifacts buried there?"

Clara leans in closer, her dark hair falling forward. "Did you find anything?"

"Just Mom's missing garden trowel." I laugh, turning the compass over in my hands. "And a very angry Dad when he saw the holes everywhere."

The weight of the compass feels right in my palm, like it belongs there. Back in middle school, while other kids plastered their walls with pop stars, mine were covered in timeline charts and maps. I'd spend hours tracing trade routes with my finger, imagining merchant ships crossing vast oceans.

"I used to drive my parents crazy," I tell Clara as I begin documenting the compass's details in our inventory system. "Every family vacation turned into a history lesson. I'd research every historical site within fifty miles of our hotel and create these elaborate itineraries."

"Complete with color-coded sticky notes," Drew adds, rolling his eyes. "Don't forget the sticky notes."

"Hey, organization is key to good research!" I defend myself, but I'm smiling. Those road trips were some of my favorite memories – Dad patiently listening to my long-winded explanations about local landmarks while Mom snapped photos of me posing in front of every historical marker we passed.

Ms. Martinez appears at my elbow, peering at the compass. "Fascinating piece. Notice the engraving along the edge? That's a maker's mark from the late 1800s."

My fingers trace the tiny letters as excitement bubbles up inside me. This is exactly why I begged Uncle James to help me get this internship. Each artifact is like a puzzle piece of the past, waiting for someone to figure out where it fits in the bigger picture.

"When I was twelve," I say, carefully placing the compass on our processing tray, "I created a mini-museum in our garage. Displayed all my 'artifacts' - mostly rocks and old bottles I'd found in the woods - with these detailed information cards I'd typed up on Mom's computer."

"Oh my god, please tell me there are pictures," Clara says, already pulling out her phone.

"Absolutely not." I reach into the box again, this time pulling out what looks like a leather-bound journal. "Though I did convince my third-grade class that a chunk of quartz I found was actually a prehistoric tool.

Got sent to the principal's office for 'spreading misinformation.'"

Drew snorts. "That's my cousin - corrupting young minds with fake artifacts since 2016."

The journal's cover is soft beneath my fingertips, worn smooth by years of handling. I've always loved how physical objects can connect us to the past. It's one thing to read about history in books, but holding something that someone actually used, touched, lived with - that makes it real.

"I used to write these elaborate stories," I continue, carefully opening the journal to its first yellowed page, "about each thing I found. Made up entire lives for the people who might have owned them. Mom said I had an overactive imagination, but I just wanted to understand the human side of history, you know?"

"We've received several boxes of donations that need proper cataloging." Ms. Martinez gestures to a collection of more cardboard boxes on a nearby table. "Remember, every object has a story waiting to be told. Your job is to help preserve those stories for future generations."

"Can we sketch them too?" Clara pulls out her drawing pad. "You know, for additional documentation?"

"That's a wonderful idea." Ms. Martinez beams. "Visual documentation can capture details that words might miss."

We head to the storage room, where the morning light filters through dusty windows, illuminating dancing particles in the air. The boxes sit like wrapped presents waiting to be opened.

"Ladies first?" Drew gestures dramatically toward the pile.

I carefully lift the lid off the first box, and the musty scent of age wafts up. Inside, wrapped in tissue paper, lies a collection of items that make my fingers tingle with anticipation.

"Oh my gosh, look at this!" I carefully lift out a vintage camera, its brass fittings dulled with time but still beautiful. The leather case is cracked but intact, telling stories of adventures long past. "Can you imagine all the moments this captured? All the memories?"

"The composition on that thing is gorgeous." Clara's already sketching, her pencil flying across the page. "Look at those art deco details around the lens."

Drew reaches into another box and pulls out a tarnished brass compass, its face scratched but still readable.

"Check this out – it's got an inscription on the back." He squints at the faded engraving. *"'To find your way home, first you must wander.'"*

"That's so poetic." I lean in for a closer look. "Though I bet whoever owned it didn't expect their wandering to lead here."

"Maybe that's exactly where they wanted it to end up." Drew balances the compass on his palm. "You know, so someone else could start their own journey."

Clara pulls out a stack of postcards tied with faded ribbon. "Speaking of journeys – looks like someone was quite the traveler. These are from all over the world!"

I carefully document each item in the museum's database, typing detailed descriptions while trying to capture every scratch, every mark that might tell part of its story. The morning flies by as we work, trading theories about who might have owned these treasures and what adventures they might have witnessed.

The camera feels warm in my hands as I photograph it from various angles, making sure to capture the manufacturer's mark and serial number. "I wonder what kind of photographer owned this. Were they a professional? Someone's grandparent documenting family memories?"

"Maybe they were a spy," Drew suggests, wiggling his eyebrows. "That's why it ended up here – too many classified secrets hidden in the film."

"In a small-town Museum of Oddities?" Clara laughs, adding shading to her sketch. "Some spy network that would be."

I carefully set the camera in its designated spot on the shelf, making sure its tag is clearly visible. "Hey, you never know. Sometimes the best stories are hidden in the most unexpected places."

As I sort through another cardboard box, my fingers brush against something leather-bound and worn. Pulling it out carefully, I discover a small scrapbook, its pages yellowed and fragile.

"Hey, check this out." I gently open it, revealing newspaper clippings meticulously arranged alongside handwritten notes in faded blue ink. "Missing Artifacts Puzzle Local Authorities," I read aloud. "Museum Mystery Remains Unsolved."

Drew peers over my shoulder. "Whoa, when's that from?"

"1973." I flip through more pages, each filled with similar headlines. "Looks like there was a string of disappearances from the museum and people's homes. All these little treasures just... vanished."

Clara abandons her sketching and slides closer. "That's wild! What kind of stuff went missing?"

"According to this, mostly personal items. A veteran's medal, someone's childhood diary, a handmade quilt..." I trail off, scanning the neat handwriting beneath each clipping.

"Nice detective work, cuz." Drew grins, expertly catching another box that threatens to topple. I watch him and Clara share an easy laugh, their natural confidence making my stomach twist slightly. They always seem so sure of themselves, while I'm here second-guessing every move.

"These notes are incredible." I focus back on the scrapbook, pushing away the familiar weight of comparison. "Whoever compiled this really did their research. There are interviews, witness statements, even theories about connections between the items."

"What kind of connections?" Clara leans in, her art forgotten.

"Well—" I begin, but Drew cuts me off.

"Hold up, what's this about missing stuff?" He points to a particular clipping.

Ms. Martinez appears beside us, her orange scarf catching the light. "Ah, I see you've found Harriet's documentation."

"Harriet?" We ask in unison.

"She was a volunteer here during that time. Absolutely brilliant at connecting dots that others missed." Ms. Martinez runs her finger along the scrapbook's spine. "These artifacts weren't just random items - they were pieces of our town's history, each with its own unique story."

My mind races with possibilities. "So someone was specifically targeting things with historical significance?"

"Not exactly." Ms. Martinez adjusts her glasses. "They seemed more interested in personal value than monetary worth. Items that meant something special to someone."

Before I can dig deeper, rapid footsteps approach our group. Mr. Chen, one of the museum assistants, hurries over with panic written across his face.

"Ms. Martinez, we have a situation." His words come out breathless. "The Wong family locket - it's gone."

"Gone?" Ms. Martinez straightens. "But that case was locked..."

"We checked the security footage." Mr. Chen wrings his hands. "Nothing unusual shows up. It's like it just... disappeared."

My heart pounds as I clutch the scrapbook tighter. The Wong family locket - I remember reading about it in the museum catalog. A delicate gold piece passed down through generations, donated just last month.

Clara gasps softly beside me. "Just like in the articles."

Drew's usual playful expression turns serious. "This can't be a coincidence."

I stare at the scrapbook in my hands, then at the empty display case visible through the storage room doorway. My mind fills with questions: *Why now? Why that specific piece? And why does it feel like history is repeating itself?*

The familiar urge to prove myself wells up inside me, but this time it's different. This isn't about measuring up to anyone else - it's about solving something real, something important.

CHAPTER 3
THE DISAPPEARANCE

I drag my feet through the museum's entrance, my stomach churning with anxiety. Yesterday's missing heirloom was bad enough, but this morning's news of a second disappearance has everyone on edge. The usual warm, inviting atmosphere feels heavy, like someone cranked up the humidity.

Drew meets me at our usual spot by the information desk, his normally casual demeanor replaced with a worried frown. "Did you hear about the second item?"

"Yeah. The vintage pocket watch, right?" I lean against the desk, watching museum staff scurry back and forth with clipboards and worried expressions.

"Yeah, Ms. Martinez is freaking out."

Clara appears beside us, her vintage dress swishing as she drops her bag. "Everyone's freaking out. I just overheard some of the board members talking about bringing in private security."

The morning light streams through the stained glass windows, casting colorful shadows across the marble floor. Usually, this sight fills me with wonder. Today, it feels like nature's trying too hard to be cheerful.

Ms. Martinez emerges from her office, her normally pristine bun slightly disheveled. She gathers all of us - staff and interns - in the main hall. The tension in the room reminds me of those moments before a big storm hits.

"As you've all heard, we've had another item go missing." Ms. Martinez's voice wavers slightly. "The pocket watch was a cherished family heirloom, and its loss deeply affects not just our museum, but our relationship with the community."

I catch Drew's eye as he mouths 'yikes.' *He's right - this is serious.*

"We need to work together," Ms. Martinez continues. "Check security footage, review visitor logs, anything that might help us understand what's happening."

My mind races back to the newspaper clippings I found yesterday. Before I can stop myself, I raise my hand. "What if we help investigate?"

The words hang in the air for a moment. Several staff members exchange glances.

"I mean," I continue, my cheeks burning, "we could talk to visitors, look for patterns, maybe find connections we're missing."

Clara perks up beside me. "I could sketch the missing items! Make flyers or something?"

"And I can check the security footage," Drew adds. "I'm pretty good with tech stuff."

Ms. Martinez considers us, her expression softening slightly. "Your enthusiasm is appreciated, but this is a serious matter."

"That's why we want to help," I press. "We know the museum, we know the exhibits. Plus, people might feel more comfortable talking to us than to security guards."

After what feels like forever, Ms. Martinez nods slowly. "Alright. But you report everything you find directly to me, understood?"

Once the meeting disperses, Drew, Clara, and I huddle near the Egyptian exhibit. The sarcophagus looms over us as we pull out our phones to take notes.

"Okay, what do we know so far?" I ask, pulling up my notes app.

Drew counts off on his fingers. "Two items missing in two days. Both family heirlooms. Both from different sections of the museum."

"And both during regular hours," Clara adds, sketching quickly in her notebook. "That's weird, right?"

"Super weird," I agree. "We should talk to the staff who work those sections first. Maybe they noticed something."

"I'll start with security footage," Drew says. "There might be something in the background we missed."

Clara holds up her sketch of the missing pocket watch. "I can talk to the art department about making these into flyers. Maybe someone saw something?"

I nod, watching another group of worried staff members hurry past. "I'll start with interviews. The more we know about when people last saw these items, the better."

My heart races with a mix of nerves and excitement as I pull out my phone's notes app. Finally, a chance to put my mystery-solving skills to use - even if those skills mostly consisted of binge-watching true crime documentaries and reading way too many Nancy Drew books.

"Remember that time we tracked down your missing necklace at school?" Clara asks, her pencil flying across her sketchpad as she works on the pocket watch drawing.

I laugh, the memory flooding back. "Oh my god, yes! We turned the whole drama department upside down looking for it."

"And it ended up being stuck in your gym locker the whole time," Clara grins, looking up from her sketch. "But hey, we found it! That totally makes us qualified detectives, right?"

"Absolutely. Two successful cases if you count the time we found your missing art portfolio under a pile of costumes."

Drew snorts, leaning against the wall next to the sarcophagus. "Wow, impressive resume. Should we get you guys badges?"

"Keep laughing," Clara tosses her eraser at him, which he catches with a grin. "But when we solve this case, you'll be begging to join our detective agency."

"Oh yeah?" Drew's eyes sparkle with amusement. "What would you call it? The Fashion Police?"

"Better than Technical Support," Clara fires back, making a show of adjusting her vintage collar. "At least we look good while solving crimes."

I flip through my notes, trying to hide my smile as they banter. "If you two are done flirting, we should probably start investigating."

They both snap their mouths shut, cheeks turning pink. Drew suddenly finds the hieroglyphics fascinating, while Clara becomes very interested in perfecting her sketch.

"So," I continue, enjoying their discomfort maybe a little too much, "I'm thinking we should split up and cover more ground. Clara, you hit up the art department for those flyers. Drew, check the security footage. I'll start with interviewing staff near where the items disappeared."

"Look at you, taking charge," Drew recovers enough to tease. "Someone's been watching too many detective shows."

"Please, I've moved on to true crime podcasts. Much more sophisticated."

Clara holds up her completed sketch. "What do you guys think? Detailed enough?"

The drawing captures every intricate detail of the missing pocket watch - the ornate engraving on the case, the slight chip on the edge that made it unique. Sometimes I forget how talented she is.

"It's perfect," Drew says, his voice softening as he studies the sketch. "You really captured all the details."

Clara beams at the compliment, tucking a strand of hair behind her ear. "Thanks! I figured the more accurate it is, the better chance someone might recognize it."

"Way better than any security camera photo," I agree. "Speaking of which, Drew, where should we start with the footage?"

He pulls out his phone, already pulling up the museum's layout. "I'm thinking we check the cameras near both theft locations first, then work our way out. See if anyone suspicious shows up in both spots."

"Ooh, like looking for a recurring character?" Clara peers over his shoulder at the screen. "That's actually pretty smart."

"Try not to sound so surprised," Drew laughs, but I notice he doesn't move away when Clara stays close.

I tap my pen against my notebook, my mind racing with possibilities. This is actually happening - we're really investigating a museum theft. Part of me wants to squeal with excitement, but I force myself to stay focused. This isn't just some game or school project. Real items are missing, items that mean something to people.

"Okay, team," I say, channeling my inner detective. "Let's meet back here in two hours to compare notes. Text if anyone finds anything suspicious."

"Yes, boss," Drew salutes mockingly.

Clara adjusts her bag on her shoulder. "I'll hit the art department first, then maybe talk to some of the guides. They might have noticed something during tours."

"Good thinking," I nod. "I'll start with the Egyptian exhibit staff since that's where the first item went missing."

My phone buzzes with another text from Drew as I flip through the dusty newspaper archives. The afternoon sun streams through the library's tall windows, casting long shadows across the wooden tables.

"Found anything yet?" Clara whispers from across the table, her dark hair falling forward as she leans in.

"Maybe." I slide my finger along a faded article. "Listen to this - 'Local resident Martha Chen reports family heirloom missing from home. Police suspect connection to museum thefts.'"

Clara and I both look up as Drew drops into the chair beside me, his usual grin replaced with concentration. "That matches what Mr. Jenkins told us about seeing someone hanging around the Asian artifacts section yesterday."

"Right?" I pull out my phone, scrolling through the notes from our staff interviews. "And get this - both times, the person was described as '*elderly*' and '*moving with purpose.*'"

"Like they knew exactly what they were looking for," Clara adds, sketching absently in her notebook. Her drawings capture the key details we've discovered - the timeline, descriptions, locations.

"But why these specific items?" Drew leans back, running a hand through his already messy hair. "The jade pendant that went missing yesterday was beautiful, but not particularly valuable."

"Just like the items from fifty years ago." I spread out more newspaper clippings. "Small things, personal things. A hand-carved box, a family photo album, a set of letters."

"Sentimental value over monetary worth." Clara's eyes light up. "What if the thief isn't after money at all?"

My heart quickens as pieces start clicking together. "The way Mr. Jenkins described the visitor - they weren't just browsing. He said they looked almost... sad."

"Like they were remembering something," Drew finishes.

I dive back into the archives with renewed purpose, scanning headlines until - "Here!" The excitement in my voice earns a stern look from the librarian. I lower my volume. "Sorry. But look at this photo."

Clara and Drew crowd around as I point to a black-and-white image. An elderly woman stands in front of the museum, clutching a small box - the same type of decorative box mentioned in the theft reports.

"Check out the inscription." Drew squints at the faded text. "'Mrs. Chen donates family heirlooms to the museum, in 1973.' Wait - Chen? Like Martha Chen from the other article?"

"The same family." My fingers trace the date. "And look who's standing next to her."

Clara gasps softly. "Is that...?"

"Ms. Martinez's mother." I can barely contain my revelation. "She was the museum curator back then."

"And now these specific items are disappearing again." Drew's voice carries a mix of concern and excitement. "Items connected to both families."

"There has to be more to this story." I carefully photograph the article and image. "Something happened between these families fifty years ago. Something that's still affecting things today."

Clara suddenly straightens. "Mei, what was the name of that staff member who reported seeing our mysterious visitor yesterday morning?"

"Um..." I check my notes. "Angela Chen. Why?"

Drew's eyes widen. "Chen. Like Martha *Chen*?"

"Her granddaughter," a quiet voice says behind us. We all jump.

Ms. Martinez stands there, her usual warm smile tinged with something sadder. Her gaze falls on the photograph spread out before us. "I see you've been doing some research."

CHAPTER 4
INVESTIGATION

I tap my pencil against the weathered pages of my research journal, staring at the growing list of missing items. The museum's usually comforting atmosphere feels heavy today, like the weight of unsolved mysteries pressing down on my shoulders.

"Look at this pattern." I slide my notebook toward Drew and Clara, who lean in close. "Every single item that's disappeared had deep personal meaning to its owner. Nothing particularly valuable in terms of money."

"Yeah, but who'd want to steal stuff that's only worth something to specific people?" Drew runs his hand through his already messy hair, making it stick up even more.

Clara adjusts her vintage cat-eye glasses, squinting at my notes. "Maybe that's exactly the point. These aren't random thefts – they're targeted for their emotional value."

My stomach does a little flip as the pieces start clicking together. "The newspaper clippings mentioned similar disappearances fifty years ago. Personal items, family heirlooms..."

"Wait." Clara's eyes light up as she flips through the old scrapbook. "Here – Margaret Anderson. She's mentioned in almost every article about the original thefts. She was really involved in documenting everything that went missing."

I lean over her shoulder, scanning the yellowed pages. "You're right. She seems to know intimate details about each stolen item."

"We should dig deeper into Margaret's story," Drew suggests, already pulling out his phone. "The library might have more records about her."

My heart races as I flip through more pages of the scrapbook, drinking in every detail about Margaret Anderson. Each word feels like another piece clicking into place, transforming this dusty old mystery into something vibrant and alive.

"Look at this." I point to a faded photograph showing a woman with kind eyes and silver-streaked hair standing in front of the museum. "That's her. She worked here as a volunteer docent for over thirty years."

Drew leans in closer, his shoulder brushing mine. "She looks exactly like someone who'd know all the museum's secrets."

"And everyone else's too," Clara adds, twirling a strand of dark hair around her finger. "Small town, long-time resident, probably knew every family's history."

I can't help bouncing my leg under the table as excitement courses through me. The more we uncover about Margaret, the more convinced I become that she's the key to understanding both the past and present disappearances. My fingers trace the careful notes she made about each missing item - a child's first baseball mitt, a handmade quilt, a grandfather's pocket watch. The details are so specific, so personal.

"She didn't just document what was stolen," I murmur, more to myself than to Drew and Clara. "She recorded the stories behind them. Why they mattered."

Clara slides closer, her vintage bangles jingling. "That's what makes this whole thing so weird, right? Like, who takes the time to learn all these intimate details about things they're stealing?"

"Unless..." Drew starts, then stops, his forehead creasing in thought.

"Unless they weren't stolen at all," I finish, the possibility hitting me like a bolt of lightning. "What if Margaret was trying to protect these items somehow?"

My mind races ahead, connecting dots I hadn't seen before. The timing of the disappearances, the careful documentation, the focus on sentimental value over monetary worth - it all points to something bigger than simple theft.

"We need to find out if Margaret is still alive," I say, pulling my laptop closer. "And if she is, we need to talk to her."

Drew's already typing on his phone. "On it. Social media might be a long shot for someone her age, but—"

"Check the local senior centers," Clara suggests, her artistic eye scanning the old photograph for more details. "That picture can't be more than twenty years old. If she was in her sixties then..."

I feel that familiar flutter of self-doubt trying to creep in - *what if we're wrong? What if this leads nowhere?* But I push it aside. Something about this feels right, feels important. The way Margaret wrote about these objects, with such care and understanding, reminds me of how I feel about the artifacts we catalog. Each one tells a story, holds a piece of someone's heart.

"Here!" Drew's voice startles me from my thoughts. "Margaret Anderson, resident at Sunnyside Senior Living. It's only fifteen minutes from here."

Clara claps her hands together. "We could go right now! The center probably has visiting hours, and—"

"Hold up," I interrupt, though I'm just as eager. "We should do this right. Let's gather everything we know about the original disappearances first. If we're going to talk to Margaret, we need to ask the right questions. Also—"

"Ms. Martinez said to report back to her," Drew said, finishing my train of thought.

I pull out fresh paper, starting a timeline of events. My hand can barely keep up with my thoughts as I jot down dates, names, and connections. This is what I love most about mysteries - the moment when chaos starts transforming into order, when random threads begin weaving themselves into a pattern.

"You've got that look," Drew says, grinning at me.

"What look?"

"The one that says you're about to crack this wide open."

I try to hide my smile but fail. He's right - I can feel it in my bones.

* * *

I lean forward in my chair, the bundle of letters spread across the library table before us. My fingers trace Margaret Anderson's elegant handwriting, each word seeming to pulse with emotion. The paper feels delicate, like it might crumble under my touch.

"Listen to this part," I say, my voice barely above a whisper. "'The items taken weren't valuable in terms of money, but they held pieces of our souls within them. Each one carried memories that can never be replaced.'"

Clara wipes her eyes with the back of her hand. "That hits different. Like, these weren't just random things to her. They were connections to people she loved."

"Yeah," Drew says, running a hand through his already-messy hair. "It's wild how something small can mean so much. Remember that beat-up baseball cap Dad gave me? The one from his first game?"

I nod, remembering how devastated Drew was when he thought he'd lost it last summer. "These letters... they're changing how I see this whole investigation. It's not just about solving a mystery anymore."

Clara pulls out her sketchbook, her eyes lighting up. "I want to draw this. Like, capture what Margaret might have felt." She starts sketching, her pencil flying across the page. "Maybe if we can visualize her story, we'll understand better what happened."

Drew scoots his chair closer to Clara's, watching her work. "That's actually brilliant. You've got such a good eye for details."

A slight blush creeps across Clara's cheeks as she continues drawing. I hide my smile, watching their interaction.

"The way Margaret describes these items," I say, shuffling through more letters. "It's like she's writing about old friends. Listen: *'Martha's music box might seem plain to others, but it played the lullaby she sang to all of us during thunderstorms. How do you replace something like that?'*"

Clara pauses her sketching, her pencil hovering above the paper. "That's beautiful and heartbreaking at the same time."

"It makes our investigation feel more important," Drew adds. "Like we're not just tracking down stolen stuff - we're trying to recover pieces of people's lives."

I feel energy coursing through me, a new determination taking hold. "These letters prove there's so much more to this mystery than we thought. Margaret knew these weren't random thefts."

Clara's sketch takes shape - a detailed drawing of Margaret as she might have looked, surrounded by meaningful objects, each one connected by delicate lines to written memories. "What do you guys think?" she asks, turning the sketchbook.

"Clara, this is incredible," I breathe, taking in the emotional depth she's captured. "You've made Margaret's story come alive."

Drew nods enthusiastically. "Seriously, you should do more of these. It helps us see the connections better."

From behind the nearby shelves, I catch snippets of conversation between two librarians.

"...just like the Anderson case..." one whispers.

"...found something in the old Thompson estate..."

My heart jumps. I grab Drew's arm, squeezing it to get his attention. Clara leans in closer, her eyes wide as we all strain to hear more.

The librarians' voices grow clearer as they move closer to our table. "...definitely connected to one of the missing pieces..."

I exchange glances with Drew and Clara, feeling my pulse quicken. Clara quietly closes her sketchbook, careful not to make any noise that might interrupt the conversation we're trying to overhear.

"Should we...?" Drew mouths, gesturing toward the librarians.

I nod slowly, gathering Margaret's letters with trembling fingers. This could be exactly what we need - a fresh lead that might help us understand both the past and present mysteries.

CHAPTER 5
HEIRLOOMS

The absent family treasure gnaws at my gut while I examine the collection of documents, snapshots, and press articles laid out before me on the table in our corner of the museum's study area. Rays of sun pierce the grimy windowpanes, throwing elongated shade patterns over our improvised research display, yet even the golden daylight fails to dispel the gloom that surrounds us.

"I can't believe another item disappeared right under our noses," I say, tapping my pencil against my notebook. "Ms. Martinez trusted us with these artifacts."

Drew leans back in his chair, running a hand through his shaggy hair. "We're doing everything we can, Mei. Sometimes mysteries take time to crack."

"Time isn't exactly on our side," Clara points out, adjusting one of the photos on our evidence board. Her vintage floral dress rustles as she moves. "Did you see how worried everyone looks? The staff keeps whispering in corners."

She's right. I've noticed the nervous glances, the hushed conversations that stop when visitors walk by. The museum's usually warm, welcoming atmosphere has shifted into something tenser, more brittle.

"Okay, let's review what we know." I pull my notebook closer, flipping through the pages of observations and theories we've collected. "The missing items aren't particularly valuable, at least not in terms of money."

"But they all have stories behind them," Drew adds, leaning forward. "That compass belonged to a local explorer, the vintage camera captured someone's wedding photos—"

"And now this heirloom," Clara interrupts, pointing to our latest addition to the board. "A family treasure passed down through generations."

Something clicks in my mind. "Wait. That's the pattern! These aren't random thefts. Each item has deep sentimental value."

Drew's eyes light up. "You're right! The thief isn't after monetary gain. They're after something more personal."

"But what's the connection?" I stand up, pacing the small space between our table and the wall of artifacts. "Why these specific items? Why now?"

Clara pulls out her sketchbook, where she's been documenting the missing items in detailed drawings. "Maybe we need to talk to more people. Visitors might have noticed something we missed."

"Good idea," Drew says. "We could set up near the entrance, ask if anyone's seen anything unusual."

I stop pacing, my mind racing with possibilities. "And what about that person hanging around the museum? The one Janet from the gift shop mentioned?"

"The one in the dark coat?" Clara asks, her pencil pausing mid-sketch. "She said they kept lingering near the displays, right?"

"Yeah, but never actually touching anything." I sit back down, pulling our witness accounts closer. "Almost like they were... waiting for something."

Drew starts organizing our notes into categories. "Or someone. What if they're connected to the original mystery? The one from fifty years ago?"

My heart speeds up at the possibility. I grab the old newspaper clippings we found, scanning them again with fresh eyes. "These thefts, they're too specific to be random. The thief knows exactly what they're looking for."

"And they know the museum's layout," Clara adds. "They'd have to, to get in and out without being caught."

A chill runs down my spine despite the warm afternoon sun. "So we're either dealing with someone who works here..."

"Or someone who's spent a lot of time studying the museum," Drew finishes my thought.

I look at our evidence board, at all the threads we've collected but haven't quite connected yet. The pressure to solve this weighs on me, but having Drew and Clara here, working through it together, makes it feel less overwhelming.

"We need to start interviewing visitors," I say, pulling out a fresh page in my notebook. "Someone must have seen something useful."

I grip my notebook tighter as I approach Mrs. Chen, one of our regular museum visitors. She's perched on her usual bench near the Victorian oddities exhibit, sketching the intricate details of a brass kaleidoscope. My heart thumps against my ribs, but I force myself to keep my voice steady.

"Mrs. Chen? Could I ask you a few questions about the museum?"

She looks up, her kind eyes crinkling behind wire-rimmed glasses. "Mei! Of course, dear. Is this about the missing items?"

"Yes." I settle beside her, flipping to a fresh page. "Have you noticed anything unusual lately? Anyone hanging around exhibits longer than normal?"

Drew catches my eye from across the room where he's talking to Mr. Peterson, an old family friend who practically lived at the museum after retiring. I give him a quick thumbs-up before turning back to Mrs. Chen.

"Now that you mention it..." She taps her pencil against her sketchbook. "There was someone last Tuesday. Kept circling back to the personal artifacts section. Seemed more interested in watching people than the exhibits."

I scribble frantically, trying to capture every detail. "Can you describe them?"

As Mrs. Chen describes a tall figure in a dark jacket, I notice Clara drifting through the exhibits with her artist's eye. She pauses near the empty space where the missing heirloom used to sit, her head tilted as she studies something I can't see.

"They asked strange questions too," Mrs. Chen continues. "Wanted to know if I remembered the old donations from the eighties. Specific ones, about family keepsakes."

My pencil freezes mid-word. "Family keepsakes?"

"Yes, like that lovely music box that disappeared last week. Such a shame – it belonged to the Williams family for generations."

Drew appears at my shoulder, his expression eager. "Mr. Peterson just told me something interesting. Remember that suspect we've been tracking? Apparently, they were asking about local history, especially about families who'd donated to the museum."

"Just like Mrs. Chen's mystery visitor," I murmur, connecting the dots in my notes.

Clara joins us, her sketchbook clutched to her chest. "Guys, I noticed something weird. All the empty spaces where items went missing? They're all in corners with limited security camera coverage. Someone really knew this place."

The tension between us crackles as we huddle together, comparing notes. What started as an exciting investigation now feels heavier, more real. I can see the strain in Drew's usually relaxed posture and hear it in Clara's quieter-than-normal voice.

"We need to organize this information better," I say, spreading my notes across an empty research table. "There has to be a pattern we're missing."

Drew runs his fingers through his hair, making it stick up even more than usual. "It's like they're collecting specific memories, not just random valuable stuff."

"Look at this." Clara opens her sketchbook, revealing detailed drawings of the empty spaces and their surroundings. "Each missing item had some kind of family connection, right? And they were all donated around the same time period."

I lean closer, studying her precise sketches. Something about the timing nags at me, but before I can chase that thought, Ms. Martinez hurries over, her face pale.

"Another item's gone missing," she says, wringing her hands. "The old pharmacy sign from the Henderson family. It was just donated last month, but it's been in their family since the 1950s."

My stomach drops as I lock eyes with Drew and Clara. This just got even more complicated, and I can feel the weight of everyone's expectations pressing down on me. But underneath the anxiety, there's a spark of determination. We're getting closer – I can feel it.

CHAPTER 6
ARTISTIC DISCOVERIES

My feet crunch along the gravel path as Drew, Clara, and I make our way to Cedar Park. The summer sun beats down, but my skin prickles with goosebumps. Another artifact disappeared this morning - this time a delicate silver locket from the Wilson family collection. We need answers, and according to our research, this park might hold them.

"Look at those oak trees," Clara points to the gnarled branches overhead. "They must be ancient. Imagine all the stories they could tell."

"If trees could talk, our job would be way easier." Drew adjusts his camera strap. "Though I bet they'd mostly complain about squirrels."

I manage a small laugh, but my mind races with connections. The park stretches before us, equal parts familiar and mysterious. I've been coming here since I was little - birthday parties, family picnics, lazy summer afternoons. But now every bench and pathway feels like it could be hiding a clue.

"We should split up," I say, pulling out my phone to check the time. "Cover more ground that way. Drew, can you check the trails? Clara, maybe scope out the pond area? I'll take the gazebo."

"Good thinking, Detective Mei." Drew shoots me finger guns before heading toward the dirt paths that wind through the trees.

"Text if you find anything interesting!" Clara calls over her shoulder, her sketchbook already in hand as she makes her way to the water.

I walk toward the white gazebo that marks the heart of the park. Its paint is peeling, revealing weathered wood underneath. This structure has been here forever - I remember Mom telling stories about coming here as a kid herself. A brass plaque catches my eye, commemorating the gazebo's construction in 1962.

Climbing the creaky steps, I run my fingers along the railing. *How many people have stood here over the decades?*

Did any of them know anything about our missing artifacts? The Wilson's locket, the museum's heirloom box, the other vanished treasures - there has to be a connection.

My stomach twists as I think about Ms. Martinez's worried face this morning. I want so badly to solve this, to prove I can handle real responsibility. *But what if I'm not good enough? What if I'm just playing detective while real items slip away?*

A cool breeze rustles through the trees, carrying Clara's voice. "Mei! Come look at this!"

I jog toward the pond where Clara crouches near the water's edge, her pencil forgotten on her sketchpad. As I get closer, I spot what caught her attention - something metallic glinting in the mud.

"Be careful," I warn as she reaches toward it. But before either of us can investigate further, Drew's shout echoes from the trails.

"Hey guys! You need to see this!"

We find Drew standing in front of a weather-worn plaque mounted on a stone marker. Moss creeps along its edges, but the text is still legible: "In memory of Elizabeth Anderson Wilson, beloved daughter of

Margaret Anderson. Her spirit lives on in this park she cherished. 1920-1975."

"Anderson?" Clara's eyes widen. "Like Margaret Anderson from the letters?"

"And Wilson," I breathe, "like the family who just lost their locket."

Drew snaps a photo of the plaque. "Think this is our missing link?"

I stare at Elizabeth's name, my heart racing. The connection feels important - too important to be a coincidence. My fingers itch to pull out my notebook and start mapping the relationships, but first, we need to document everything we've found.

"Clara, what exactly did you see by the pond?" I ask, already walking back toward the water.

I let out a deep breath as Drew and Clara approach the gazebo where I've been waiting. The wooden structure creaks beneath our feet as we gather, its weathered boards holding decades of stories – and hopefully some answers.

"You guys won't believe what I found," Clara bursts out, her eyes sparkling with excitement. She pulls something from her pocket, holding it up to catch the afternoon light filtering through the latticed roof.

"What is that?" I lean forward, studying the small metallic object dangling from her fingers. A tarnished locket, its surface dulled by time and exposure.

"I spotted it near the pond," Clara explains, carefully placing it in my outstretched palm. "It was half-buried in the dirt, but something made me look twice."

Drew peers over my shoulder. "Can you open it?"

My fingers trace the edge until I find the tiny clasp. It takes a few tries, but finally, the locket springs open. Inside, barely visible through years of tarnish, I make out an inscription: "To Margaret, with love eternal - 1973."

"Margaret?" I gasp. "As in Margaret Anderson?"

"No way." Drew pulls out his phone, fingers flying across the screen. "Let me cross-reference this with what we found at the library."

"The timing matches," I say, excitement building in my chest. "This could be exactly what we need – proof that connects the missing heirloom to the park's history."

Clara starts pacing, her creative energy practically radiating off her. "But why here? Why would Margaret's locket end up by the pond after all these years?"

"Maybe it wasn't lost," Drew suggests, still scrolling through his phone. "Maybe it was hidden."

The weight of what we might have stumbled upon settles over us. I close my eyes, trying to piece it all together, but frustration bubbles up instead.

"I just wish people would take us seriously," I blurt out. "We're not just kids playing detective. We're actually onto something here."

Clara stops pacing. "Mei, we're all feeling the pressure, but maybe we need to slow down. What if we mess this up?"

"Mess it up?" My voice rises slightly. "We've already found more leads than anyone else. Why are you suddenly doubting us?"

"I'm not doubting us!" Clara's face flushes. "I just don't want to disappoint everyone if we can't solve this!"

"Hey, time out." Drew steps between us, his usual easygoing expression replaced with concern. "Look at what we've already accomplished together. Clara, your artistic eye spotted this locket when anyone else would have walked right past it. Mei, your instincts about the historical connections have been spot-on. And me? I'm pretty good at keeping you both from strangling each other."

Despite myself, I crack a smile. "You're right. I'm sorry, Clara. I guess I'm just scared of letting everyone down."

Clara's expression softens. "Me too. And I hate feeling that way because you guys mean everything to me."

"Group hug?" Drew suggests, already pulling us both in.

As we embrace, something clicks in my mind. "Wait – the locket, the old records – didn't we read something about Margaret's family living in that Victorian house on Maple Street?"

"The one with the blue shutters?" Clara pulls back, eyes wide. "It's only a few blocks from here!"

Drew's already pulling up a map on his phone. "If Margaret lived there, maybe that's where we'll find our next clue."

CHAPTER 7
SEARCHING FOR CLUES

I grip the locket tighter in my pocket as we make our way down Cedar Street, the setting sun painting everything in shades of amber and gold. My legs feel heavy after our long day at the park, but the weight of our discovery pushes me forward. Drew walks beside me, his usual swagger replaced by an intense focus I rarely see in my cousin. Clara trails just behind, her sketchbook tucked under her arm, occasionally stopping to jot down quick notes.

"That has to be it," I say, pointing to a Victorian-style house looming at the end of the street. The peeling yellow paint and sagging shutters make it look like a forgotten postcard from another era. "Number 442."

"Definitely gives off mysterious vibes," Drew says, running a hand through his messy hair. "Like something straight out of your mystery novels, Mei."

I shoot him a look. "Thanks for the confidence boost."

The grass has grown wild around the property, pushing through cracks in the concrete pathway. Discarded newspapers lie scattered across the porch, their pages yellow and brittle. The whole scene makes my stomach twist - not with fear exactly, but with an overwhelming sense that we're about to stumble onto something bigger than ourselves.

Clara steps up beside me, her artistic eye taking in every detail. "Look at those windows - the way they're designed, it's like they're watching us. I bet this place was gorgeous back in the day."

We reach the porch steps, and each creak under our feet sends my heart racing a little faster. The wooden boards feel solid enough, but decades of neglect have left their mark. Standing before the front door, reality crashes over me.

"What if we're wrong?" I whisper, voicing the doubt that's been gnawing at me. "What if this is just another dead end?"

Drew places a reassuring hand on my shoulder. "Then we'll find another lead. But you're the one who connected the dots, Mei. Trust your instincts."

"He's right," Clara adds, pulling out her phone to snap a few reference photos. "Besides, that locket didn't end up in the park by accident. Everything's connected somehow."

I take a deep breath, drawing strength from their confidence. The late afternoon light streams through the trees, casting strange shadows across the wraparound porch. Wind chimes hanging from a rusty hook tinkle softly, their melody somehow both melancholic and hopeful.

"Okay," I say, squaring my shoulders. "Clara, you mentioned wanting to check the attic? Those usually have the best family treasures."

She nods, clutching her sketchbook closer. "The light up there should be perfect for sketching any clues we find."

"I'll take the living room," Drew volunteers, already peering through a grimy window. "Looks like there might be some old photo albums or something."

"Then I'll start with the kitchen." I pull out my own notebook, ready to document everything. "Meet back here in thirty minutes? And guys..." I pause, making eye contact with both of them. "Be careful. This place feels...important."

We share a moment of understanding, the weight of our investigation settling around us like the dust that coats everything in sight. As I reach for the tarnished doorknob, my fingers trembling slightly, I can't shake the feeling that whatever we find inside will change everything.

The door creaks open, releasing a wave of musty air that smells like old books and forgotten memories. Floorboards groan under our careful steps as we enter, and I have to fight the urge to hold my breath. Shafts of sunlight cut through the darkness, illuminating swirling dust motes that dance around us like tiny constellations.

"Like stepping into a time capsule," Clara whispers, her eyes wide as she takes in the sheet-covered furniture and faded wallpaper.

Drew pulls out his phone's flashlight, the beam cutting through the shadows. "Where stories go to sleep," he murmurs, uncharacteristically poetic.

I squeeze the locket once more for luck, then pull out my own flashlight. "Okay, team. Let's see what secrets this place is hiding."

* * *

I step into the dimly lit kitchen, dust motes dancing in the thin rays of sunlight that pierce through grimy windows. The space feels frozen in time, with its vintage appliances and faded wallpaper peeling at the corners. My footsteps echo against the worn linoleum floor as I move toward a set of cabinets.

"So much dust," I murmur, running my finger along a counter edge. Years of accumulated grime come away on my fingertip.

In the corner, tucked beneath a built-in breakfast nook, I spot a wooden box. My heart skips as I crouch down to examine it. The brass clasp is tarnished but intact, and the wood feels smooth beneath my hands despite its age. With careful movements, I ease open the lid.

Inside, I find a collection of family heirlooms - delicate pieces of the past preserved in this forgotten corner. A tablecloth catches my eye, its once-white fabric now yellowed with age. The intricate lacework along its edges speaks of countless family gatherings, holidays, and celebrations.

"Just like the ones Mom keeps in our china cabinet," I whisper, thinking of how she preserves our own family treasures. But these items feel different - weightier somehow. They belong to a family with deep roots here, generations of history woven into every thread.

My throat tightens as I lift the tablecloth, revealing more items beneath. A silver serving spoon. A collection of handwritten recipe cards. Each piece tells a story of family traditions and careful preservation. Unlike me, stumbling through this investigation, these people knew exactly who they were and what mattered to them.

From the living room, I hear Drew call out, "Guys, you need to see this!"

"Coming!" I carefully fold the tablecloth and place it back in the box, my thoughts still swirling with doubt. These artifacts belonged to people who built lasting legacies. Meanwhile, I can barely figure out the mystery in front of me.

"Hold up," Clara's voice drifts down from the attic. "I found something too!"

I carry the box with me as I head toward Drew's voice, my footsteps hesitant on the creaking floorboards. When I enter the living room, he's kneeling by an old trunk, surrounded by black and white photographs spread across the floor.

"Look at these," Drew says, holding up a photograph. "It's them - the original owners."

The image shows a happy family gathered around a dinner table, the same tablecloth I just found draped beneath their feast. My chest tightens at their bright smiles, the obvious love connecting them across time.

Clara appears in the doorway, clutching what looks like an old sketchbook. Her eyes are bright with excitement. "The attic is full of treasures. You won't believe what I found up there."

Before she can continue, a distinct creak echoes from somewhere deeper in the house. We freeze, exchanging wide-eyed looks. Another creak follows, closer this time.

"Did you guys hear that?" I whisper, my heart hammering against my ribs.

Drew nods slowly, and Clara edges closer to us. The sounds are unmistakable now - footsteps, moving through another room in the supposedly empty house.

I grip the box tighter, my mind racing. *Someone else* is here with us, and based on the missing artifacts from the museum, I have a feeling this isn't a coincidence.

CHAPTER 8
A LOCAL HISTORIAN

My heart pounds against my ribs as we stand frozen in the hallway, straining to hear more of the mysterious sounds drifting from the next room. Drew's shoulder presses against mine, and I can feel Clara's quick breaths behind us. The late afternoon sun casts long shadows through grimy windows, making every corner of this old house feel alive with secrets.

"We need to check it out," I whisper, surprised by the steadiness in my voice. "But we stick together, okay?"

Drew nods, his usual playful demeanor replaced by focused determination. "Right behind you, cuz."

"I don't love this," Clara murmurs, but she grips my arm

in solidarity. "But you're right – we can't leave without knowing."

We inch forward, and I wince at every tiny creak beneath our feet. The floorboards seem determined to announce our presence, no matter how carefully we step. The sound grows clearer – shuffling papers, something heavy being moved, the distinct thud of objects being set aside.

At the door, Drew reaches past me for the brass knob. "Let me just..." He turns it with agonizing slowness, pushing the door open just enough for a sliver of visibility. The hinges protest with a soft whine that makes my stomach flip.

Through the gap, I see a room cluttered with sheet-covered furniture and stacked boxes. Dust motes dance in weak rays of sunlight streaming through a partially boarded window. The air smells musty and stale, like forgotten memories.

That's when we spot the figure.

They're hunched over an old trunk in the corner, methodically removing items and examining them before setting them aside. Even in the dim light, I can make out weathered hands moving with purpose.

Clara's fingers dig into my shoulder as she stifles a gasp. My mind races – *should we run? Confront them? Call someone?*

But curiosity wins out. I push the door wider, wincing at the creak that seems to echo through the empty house. The figure stiffens, then slowly turns toward us.

Recognition hits me like a physical force. "Mrs. Chen?"

The elderly woman blinks at us, her hand pressed to her chest. *I know her* – she's visited the museum several times, always asking detailed questions about the exhibits' histories. She's written several books about local families and their stories.

"Oh my," she breathes, straightening up with one hand steadying herself against the trunk. "You gave me quite a start." Her eyes dart between the three of us, a mix of surprise and something else – *guilt? Concern?* "Though I suppose I should be asking what brings three young people to this old place?"

Drew steps forward, positioning himself slightly in front of me and Clara. "We could ask you the same thing, Mrs. Chen. Why are you going through these things?"

She looks down at the items scattered around her feet – old photos, letters, small trinkets that catch what little light filters into the room. "I suppose," she says slowly, "we might all be here for similar reasons."

My mind whirls with possibilities. *Could she be connected to the missing artifacts? Or is she simply doing research for another book?* The historian in her would certainly be drawn to an old house like this, but something about her demeanor suggests there's more to the story.

"The museum's missing items," I say, watching her face carefully. "Do you know anything about them?"

Her expression shifts, subtle but noticeable. Recognition flickers in her eyes, and she sets down the photograph she's holding with trembling fingers. "Perhaps," she says carefully, "we should have a proper conversation about that."

Mrs. Chen, the local historian who occasionally gives talks at the museum about our town's past. Relief floods through me, though my muscles remain tense.

"I didn't expect anyone else to be here," Mrs. Chen says softly, her hands trembling slightly as she steps away from the trunk. "This was my grandmother's house, you see. I come here sometimes, just to remember."

Drew clears his throat beside me. "Mrs. Chen, we're actually here investigating some missing items from the museum. We apologize for trespassing."

She settles onto a nearby chair, dust puffing up around her. "It's alright, dear," she said, getting comfortable. "They're connected to this place more than you know. My grandmother's family - the Wangs - they lived here for generations. That pearl-inlaid music box that disappeared? It belonged to my great-aunt."

Clara pulls out her sketchbook, her pencil already moving across the page. "Would you tell us more about your family? I'd love to capture some of these stories."

"Stories are all we have left sometimes," Mrs. Chen says, watching Clara sketch. "That music box played at every family celebration for decades. When my great-grandmother passed, it was supposed to go to her youngest daughter. But there was a dispute..."

I sink to the floor near her feet, my earlier fears forgotten. "I understand about family legacies. My mom always says objects carry memories, like echoes of the past."

Mrs. Chen's eyes light up. "Exactly, dear. Here, let me show you something." She turns back to the trunk, her fingers finding a hidden catch along its edge. With a soft click, a compartment springs open.

"Secret compartments were common in old family trunks," she explains, carefully removing a bundle of letters tied with faded ribbon. "These might help explain what happened back then - and maybe even now."

My hands shake slightly as I accept the letters. The paper is delicate and yellowed with age. As I carefully unfold the first one, the scent of old paper and ink fills my nose.

"These mention the original thefts," I say, scanning the neat handwriting. "Your great-aunt wrote about losing family treasures, how it tore relationships apart."

Drew leans over my shoulder to read. "Look at this part - she talks about items going missing right after big arguments, like someone was taking revenge."

Clara pauses her sketching. "Just like what's happening now. The missing items all belonged to families with deep roots in the community."

Mrs. Chen nods slowly. "History has a way of repeating itself. Perhaps I could help you understand more at the museum? These letters might make more sense in context with what else you've found."

I gather the letters carefully, excitement building in my chest. This could be exactly what we need to crack the case. For the first time since starting this investigation, I feel truly confident about our direction.

"We'd really appreciate that," I start to say, but freeze as distinct footsteps crunch on the gravel outside the house.

CHAPTER 9
THE INTRUDER

My heart threatens to burst through my chest as the footsteps grow louder. I press my back against the worn wallpaper, feeling every breath like thunder in my ears. Drew catches my eye from his hiding spot behind a massive bookcase, his usual easy smile replaced with tight concentration. Clara's barely visible behind a dusty armchair, her sketchbook clutched to her chest.

The elderly woman - Mrs. Chen, she'd introduced herself minutes ago - crouches beside me, her wrinkled hand finding mine in the shadows. The warmth of her grip steadies my racing thoughts.

"Should be empty," a voice mutters from the hallway. Female. Familiar in a way I can't quite place.

The floorboards protest under slow, deliberate steps. I hold my breath as a shadow stretches across the doorway, followed by a figure that makes my eyes widen. *It's her* - the guy who's been hanging around the museum displays, always vanishing just as staff approach. In the dim light filtering through grimy windows, his features are sharp with purpose.

She moves straight to the trunk we were just examining, completely unaware of our presence. Her movements are quick but careful as he rifles through the contents, muttering under his breath.

"Has to be here somewhere... they wouldn't have moved it..."

Drew shifts slightly, and a small cloud of dust rises from the floorboards. I freeze, but our intruder is too focused on her search to notice. Clara's fingers twitch toward her pencil - even now, her artist's instinct wants to capture the moment.

The urge to leap out and demand answers burns in my throat. This could be our chance to solve everything - the missing heirlooms, the connection to the past, all of it. Mrs. Chen squeezes my hand again, as if sensing my thoughts.

I lean close to Drew, my whisper barely a breath. "We need to confront her. She might have answers about the artifacts."

"It's risky," Drew mouths back, but I see the spark of adventure in his eyes.

Clara catches our exchange and nods firmly, already sliding her sketchbook into her bag. We've come too far to back down now.

I take a deep breath, mentally running through everything we've learned. The family letters, the mysterious thefts, the pattern of sentimental items vanishing - it all has to connect somehow. And this woman, frantically searching through decades-old memories, might be the key to understanding why.

"Ready?" I mouth to my friends, receiving determined nods in response.

Mrs. Chen's grip tightens on my hand one last time before letting go. Her eyes hold a mixture of worry and encouragement that reminds me of my mom.

The stranger's frustration grows audible as she tosses aside old photographs and papers. "Where did they put it? The ledger has to be here somewhere…"

I catch Drew's eye again, tilting my head toward the center of the room. He understands immediately, positioning himself to block the doorway if needed. Clara shifts too, ready to move from her hiding spot.

My heart pounds against my ribs as I prepare to step out. Everything we've investigated, every clue we've gathered, has led to this moment. I straighten my shoulders, gathering every ounce of courage I can muster.

The floorboard creaks under my foot as I move, and the stranger's head snaps up.

My heart pounds against my ribs as I step out from behind the dusty bookcase.

"I know who you are," I say, my voice steadier than I feel. "And I want to know what you're doing with the missing items from the museum."

The suspect - a middle-aged woman with dark hair tied back in a messy bun - clutches an old leather-bound book to her chest. Her shoulders slump slightly.

"You're the new intern," she says softly. "The one who's been asking questions."

Drew and Clara emerge from their hiding spots, flanking me. Mrs. Chen joins us—her presence somehow makes me feel braver.

"Those items belong to my family," the woman continues, her voice cracking. "They were taken from us years ago - stolen really, through legal loopholes and false claims. I've spent years tracking them down."

"Why didn't you just come forward?" Clara asks, her artistic sensitivity picking up on the woman's pain.

"Would anyone have believed me? After all this time?" She shakes her head. "I tried proper channels before. Nobody listened."

The elderly historian steps forward, recognition dawning on her face. "Lizabeth, is that you? I remember your grandmother speaking about this."

The suspect - Lizabeth - nods, tears welling in her eyes. "You knew my grandmother?"

"I was there when it happened," Mrs. Chen says. "The way your family's treasures were scattered... it wasn't right."

I feel the tension in the room shift as understanding blooms. Drew moves closer to me, his presence reassuring.

"We can help," I offer. "If what you're saying is true, we can work together to make this right. But taking things without explanation only makes it worse."

Lizabeth wipes her eyes with the back of her hand. "I didn't know who to trust. Every time I tried to explain…"

"Show us," Clara interrupts gently. "Show us the proof you have. We can help document everything, create a proper chain of evidence."

"The museum has archives," Drew adds. "Records that could support your claim if we look carefully enough."

Lizabeth hesitates, then slowly opens the leather book she's holding. Inside are photographs, newspaper clippings, and handwritten letters - a family's history carefully preserved.

"This is everything I've gathered over the years," she explains. "Proof of ownership, family stories, documentation of how things were lost."

The elderly historian peers at the materials, nodding. "Yes, yes. I remember some of these pieces. Your grandmother's jade collection was particularly beautiful."

I feel a surge of excitement as pieces of the puzzle start fitting together. "If we work together, we can present this properly to Ms. Martinez. She'll listen if we have evidence."

"We need to be careful though," Drew cautions. "Do this the right way this time."

Clara pulls out her sketchbook. "I can help document everything visually. Create a timeline."

My mind races with possibilities as we gather around Lizabeth's book, five unlikely allies brought together by decades-old secrets. But before we can dive deeper into our planning, a loud creak echoes from the front door. We all freeze, exchanging alarmed looks as heavy footsteps sound in the entrance hall.

I grab Drew's arm instinctively, my earlier confidence wavering as the footsteps grow closer. Lizabeth clutches her book tighter, while Clara holds her breath beside me. Mrs. Chen's face pales as we wait, trapped in this dusty room with nowhere to hide.

Who else was looking for clues?

CHAPTER 10
COMMON GROUND

My heart pounds against my ribs as the door's creak echoes through the dusty halls of the old family home. Everyone around me freezes - Drew, Clara, Mrs. Chen, and even our newfound ally, Lizabeth, the suspect we'd just confronted. The sound hangs in the air like suspended dust motes catching the late afternoon light.

"Quick," I whisper, gesturing toward the heavy Victorian furniture scattered throughout the room. "Hide."

Drew slides behind a towering bookcase, while Clara and Mrs. Chen duck behind a massive rolled-arm sofa. Our former suspect - who'd just revealed their connection to the missing heirlooms - crouches beside an antique chest. I press myself against the wall behind a heavy velvet curtain, its musty fabric tickling my nose.

"Stay absolutely still," I breathe out, barely audible. My fingers grip the curtain's thick material as footsteps approach, each one making the floorboards groan under their weight.

The door swings open wider, and through a gap in the curtain, I watch a man step into the room. He's tall, maybe in his fifties, wearing a weathered jacket and carrying what looks like an old leather satchel. Something about him seems familiar, though I can't place why. His movements are purposeful as he scans the room, reminding me of the descriptions I'd heard from the museum staff about a suspicious visitor who'd been asking oddly specific questions about the exhibits.

He begins pulling open drawers and rifling through papers, muttering under his breath. The sound of shuffling documents fills the room as he grows increasingly agitated with each empty drawer.

"Has to be here somewhere," he growls, slamming a drawer shut. "Those pieces belonged to us, not them. Never should've ended up in that museum in the first place."

I catch Drew's eye across the room. His expression mirrors my thoughts - this man knows something about the missing artifacts. The elderly woman clutches Clara's hand, both of them barely breathing as the man continues his search.

"Generations of memories," he continues, his voice rising with frustration. "Family history just... given away like it meant nothing. Like we meant nothing." He kicks at a stack of boxes, sending them tumbling. "Father should've never let them take it. Should've fought harder."

My mind races, connecting dots. The way he talks about family history, the bitterness in his voice - it matches perfectly with the pattern we've been uncovering. Each missing item has been tied to deep family connections, to stories of loss and separation.

The man pulls out an old photograph from his satchel, holding it up to the dim light. "See what you've done?" he says to the image. "All scattered now. Broken apart. But I'll get them back. Every last piece."

I press myself flatter against the wall as he moves closer to my hiding spot. Through the curtain's gap, I can see the photograph trembling in his hand - it shows a family gathered around what looks like one of the missing heirlooms from the museum. The same one that had disappeared just days ago.

Clara shifts slightly behind the sofa, causing the floorboard to creak. The man whirls around, stuffing the photograph back into his satchel. "Who's there?" he demands, voice sharp with suspicion.

We all hold our breath, frozen in our hiding spots. The air feels electric with tension as he takes slow, deliberate steps toward the sofa. I can see Clara's fingers whitening as she grips the elderly woman's hand tighter, both of them pressing themselves deeper into the shadows.

The man pauses, his back to me, head cocked as if listening for any sound that might give us away. Drew catches my eye again, his hand inching toward a heavy brass candlestick on the shelf beside him. I give him the smallest shake of my head - we can't risk confrontation, not when we might learn more by staying hidden.

I stand frozen, my heart hammering against my ribs as I watch the intruder continue his frantic search through the room. Drew catches my eye from his hiding spot behind a dusty armchair, and I give him a slight nod. We can't stay hidden forever – not when answers might be within our grasp.

"We need to approach this carefully," I whisper to Clara, who's crouched beside me.

She squeezes my hand, her presence steadying my nerves. The elderly woman – Mrs. Chen – signals her readiness from behind a tall bookcase.

Taking a deep breath, I step out from our hiding place, my voice steadier than I feel. "Looking for something specific?"

The man whirls around, nearly knocking over a stack of old books. His face drains of color as Drew, Clara, Mrs. Chen, and Lizabeth all emerge from their hiding spots. He backs up against the trunk he'd been searching, his hands raised defensively.

"This isn't what it looks like," he stammers.

"Really? Because it looks like you're searching for the same things we are." I take another step forward, emboldened by my friends' presence. "The missing artifacts from the museum?"

He starts to protest, but Mrs. Chen cuts him off. "Thomas Reynolds," she says, her voice thick with recognition. "I should have known you'd come here."

The man – Thomas – stares at her in shock. "How do you—"

"I knew your grandmother, Margaret." Mrs. Chen's words silence the room. "She used to talk about these heirlooms all the time."

Something shifts in Thomas's expression – pain, maybe, or longing. "Then you know why I need to find them. They never should have left our family."

"We're not here to stop you," I say, surprising myself with the certainty in my voice. "We want to understand. These disappearances, the connections to fifty years ago – it all means something, doesn't it?"

Thomas sinks onto a nearby chair, the fight draining from his posture. "My grandmother... she lost everything. The museum, the town – they took pieces of our history, claimed them for public display without understanding what they meant to us."

Drew steps forward. "The photograph I found earlier – that was your grandmother, wasn't it? With the missing locket?"

"Yes," Thomas nods. "One of many things that should have stayed in the family."

Clara pulls out her sketchbook, flipping to a drawing she made of the recently missing items. "Everything that's disappeared – they're all connected to your family?"

"Most of them." Thomas leans forward, studying her sketches. "But there are still pieces missing."

Mrs. Chen joins us, her eyes bright with understanding. "We can help each other, Thomas. Between your knowledge, these young people's investigation skills, and my memories of that time – we might be able to make things right."

I feel the energy in the room shift as possibility replaces suspicion. "The museum archives," I say excitedly. "If we work together, we could—"

A sharp ringtone cuts through the air, making us all jump. Thomas's hand moves to his pocket, where his phone glows through the fabric of his jacket. The screen illuminates his startled face as the ringing continues, loud and insistent in the sudden silence.

CHAPTER 11
GATHERING INFO

I stand frozen, my heart hammering against my ribs as the man's phone pierces the dusty silence of the old house. The sharp ringtone feels like an alarm, warning us that our careful plans might shatter. Drew shifts closer to me, while Clara's fingers brush against my arm - a silent reminder that we're in this together.

The man yanks his phone from his pocket, his face draining of color as he checks the screen. His earlier bravado crumbles, replaced by something that looks suspiciously like fear. I've seen that look before - on my own face in the mirror when I'm caught in a situation I can't control.

"I need to take this," he mutters, stepping away from us. His shoes leave marks in the dust as he paces, hunched over the phone like it might bite him.

Mrs. Chen - I still can't believe we found her here - catches my eye and shakes her head slightly. Something about this call has her worried too. I lean in closer to Drew and Clara, keeping my voice barely above a whisper. "We should listen."

Through the musty air, fragments of conversation drift our way. "No, I haven't... the museum situation is... we're running out of..." Each snippet makes my stomach twist tighter. The museum - *our museum* - keeps coming up, and the way he says it makes me think there's more at stake than just missing family heirlooms.

Clara squeezes my hand, her artist's fingers trembling slightly. Drew's shoulders are tense as he tracks the man's movement across the room. The floorboards creak under the stranger's nervous pacing, and dust motes dance in the dying sunlight streaming through grimy windows.

"What do you think he's talking about?" Clara breathes against my ear.

I shake my head, straining to catch more details. The man's voice grows more agitated with each passing second. His free hand rakes through his hair, leaving it standing on end. Whatever news he's receiving, it's not good.

"Time's running out," he snaps into the phone, loud enough for all of us to hear clearly. "If we don't get those items back to the—" His eyes dart to us, and he lowers his voice again, turning away.

My mind races. *Items back to where? Who's on the other end of that call?* Mrs. Chen steps forward, her eyes narrowing as she watches the man. There's recognition in her expression - she knows something about this situation that we don't.

The call ends abruptly, and the man shoves his phone back into his pocket. His shoulders slump as he braces himself against the wall, muttering under his breath. The tension in the room feels thick enough to cut.

I exchange a quick glance with Drew and Clara before stepping forward. We've come too far to back down now. "Who was that?" I demand, surprised by the steadiness in my voice. "What's really going on at the museum?"

The man turns, and the look on his face stops me cold. Gone is the defensive stranger we confronted earlier. In his place stands someone who looks haunted, desperate even. "You kids don't understand what you've stumbled into."

"Then help us understand," Drew says, moving to stand beside me. Clara follows, and the elderly woman completes our semicircle around him. We've got him cornered, but something tells me he might actually want to talk now.

"The museum situation," I press, "what did you mean about running out of time? What's really happening to those missing items?"

His eyes dart between us, calculating. I can practically see the wheels turning in his head as he weighs his options. The silence stretches, broken only by the settling of the old house around us and our collective breath held in anticipation.

Finally, he pushes himself away from the wall, shoulders squared. "This isn't just about family heirlooms anymore," he says, voice heavy with resignation. "There's something bigger happening at that museum, something that started fifty years ago. And now..." He pauses, checking his phone again before looking back at us with an intensity that makes me shiver. "Now we might be too late to stop it."

***

My heart pounds against my ribs as the man before us runs his hand through his graying hair, anxiety etched across his weathered face. The phone call clearly rattled him, and now he paces the dusty floor of the old house like a caged animal.

"Look, there's something bigger going on here," he finally says, stopping to face us. "These items—they're not just family heirlooms. People are trying to sell them on the black market."

"The black market?" I exchange glances with Drew and Clara. "But why would anyone want—"

"Because they're part of this town's legacy," he cuts in, his voice dropping to almost a whisper. "Each piece tells a story about the founding families, about secrets some people would rather keep buried."

Mrs. Chen steps forward, her eyes sharp with recognition. "The Morrison compass," she says. "And the Richardson family letters. They're all connected to the town charter, aren't they?"

The man nods grimly. "Among other things. I've been tracking these items for years, trying to keep them from disappearing forever."

"Then we need to work together," I say, surprised by the strength in my voice. "We all want the same thing—to protect these artifacts and their history."

Clara pulls out her sketchbook, flipping to a fresh page. "I can map out the connections between the families and the items. Maybe we'll spot a pattern we missed before."

"And I know every hidden corner of this town's history," Mrs. Chen adds, a slight smile crossing her face. "The stories that never made it into the official records."

The man hesitates, then pulls out his phone. "I have leads—places where these items might show up. Underground collectors, private auctions."

"We should split up," I suggest, my mind racing with possibilities. "Cover more ground before the museum closes. Drew and I can check the locations closest to downtown. Clara, you and Mrs.—"

"Call me Martha," the elderly woman interjects.

"Martha can investigate the historical angle. And you—" I turn to the man, realizing I still don't know his name.

"James," he supplies. "James Morrison."

My eyebrows shoot up at the familiar surname, but

there's no time to unpack that connection. "You can use your contacts to monitor any potential sales."

Everyone nods in agreement, and we quickly exchange phone numbers. The energy in the room has shifted from tense suspicion to focused determination. As we gather our things, Martha shares a story about the Morrison compass's role in mapping the original town boundaries, adding another layer to our understanding of its significance.

"Meet back at the museum in two hours," I say, checking my phone. "That gives us time before closing to compare notes."

Drew shoulders his backpack. "This is *way* bigger than we thought, isn't it?"

"Sometimes the smallest things hold the biggest secrets," Martha says, patting his arm.

We make our way out of the house and onto the sidewalk, the late afternoon sun casting long shadows across the pavement. As we walk toward the museum, James fills us in on more details about the black market for historical artifacts, while Martha connects his information to local legends I've never heard before.

The museum comes into view, its brick facade familiar and somehow different now that I know what's at stake. That's when I spot them—a figure in dark clothing, pressed against the window, peering inside with obvious intent.

We all freeze mid-step. The figure hasn't noticed us yet, too focused on whatever they're looking for inside the building. My pulse races as I feel Drew tense beside me, and Clara's sharp intake of breath cuts through the silence.

Where did Lizabeth go?

CHAPTER 12
HUSHED TONES

Could this Victorian house get any weirder?

My heart pounds against my ribs as I crouch behind a sculpted hedge, eyes fixed on the shadowy figure peering through the museum's windows. Drew's shoulder presses against mine, and I feel Clara's quick breaths behind us. Mrs. Chen – Martha, as she introduced herself – and the man we met at the house, Mr. Morrison, remain a few steps behind, their whispered theories barely reaching my ears. *Where did Martha go to?*

"They're definitely casing the place," Drew mutters, his usual playful tone replaced with steel. "Look at how they keep checking over their shoulder."

I nod, studying the figure's movements. They seem almost familiar with the building's layout, moving from window to window with purpose. "We need to be smart about this. If they're involved in selling the artifacts, they might not be alone."

Clara grips my arm, her artistic hands steady despite the tension. "What if we split up? Create a distraction at the front while someone checks the back entrance?"

"That could work," I whisper, memories of the past few weeks flooding my mind – cataloging artifacts, discovering clues, forming unexpected alliances. The weight of everything we've uncovered settles on my shoulders, but instead of crushing me, it strengthens my resolve.

Mrs. Chen's gentle voice carries from behind us. "Those artifacts aren't just items to be sold. Each piece holds generations of memories, of love, of loss." Her words catch slightly. "The silver music box that went missing? I remember my grandmother playing it every Sunday evening while telling stories of our family's journey to this town."

Mr. Morrison nods solemnly. "We can't let them disappear into private collections. They belong here, where their stories can be shared."

I take a deep breath, formulating a plan. "Drew, you and Clara take the west side. There's that maintenance entrance near the loading dock. Mrs. Chen, Mr. Morrison – you approach from the front. Act like you're just leaving for the day. I'll circle around to the east entrance. Oh, and did you see where Lizabeth went?"

"Mei," Drew's concern bleeds through his whisper, "are you sure about splitting up?"

"We need to cover all exits," I respond, surprising myself with my confidence. "Besides, we're not really alone – we've got each other's backs. Have you seen Lizabeth?" I whisper to him.

Drew looks around the area and shakes his head, no.

We move like shadows across the grounds. The setting sun casts long fingers of light between the buildings, creating perfect covers of darkness. Drew and Clara disappear around one corner while I press myself against the cool brick wall, inching toward the east side.

Mrs. Chen's voice rings out clear and strong, startling the figure. "Oh my! I didn't expect anyone else here!"

The figure whirls around, and I catch a glimpse of their face in the fading light. They're younger than I expected, maybe in their thirties, with sharp features and calculating eyes.

"The house is vacant," they snap, trying to sound authoritative despite being caught off guard.

Mr. Morrison steps forward, his presence commanding attention. "Funny, I was about to say the same thing. But then again, I don't suppose vacancy matters much when you're planning to fence stolen artifacts."

The figure's posture changes instantly – defensive, coiled like a spring. "You don't know what you're talking about. These items were never meant to be locked away in display cases. They belong with the families who—"

"Who what?" Mrs. Chen interrupts, her voice carrying years of history and hurt. "Who would sell them to the highest bidder? Who would tear them away from the community that cherishes them?"

I position myself near the gate entrance, ready to move if they try to run. Through the twilight, I spot Drew and Clara mirroring my stance on the opposite side. The figure glances between them, realizing they're surrounded, and their façade begins to crack.

"You don't understand," they say, and for the first time, I

hear something beyond greed in their voice – something that sounds almost like pain.

"Those artifacts aren't yours to sell," I call out, my voice steadier than I feel. "They belong to our community, to our families."

Drew steps forward, his presence reassuring beside me. "We know about the black market deals. It stops now."

The figure—a middle-aged man with graying temples—backs up against the museum wall. "You don't understand. These items were stolen from my family decades ago. I'm just reclaiming what's mine."

Clara's artistic eye catches something I almost miss. "Your hands," she points out. "They're stained with the same preservation chemicals we use in the museum. You've been handling the artifacts recently."

Mrs. Chen moves closer, her eyes narrowing. "I remember you. You're Thomas Reynolds' grandson, aren't you? Your grandfather helped establish this museum."

"And they pushed him out!" the man spits, anger flashing across his face. "Took everything he'd collected and displayed it like it was theirs."

"That's not true," the elderly woman counters. "I was there. Your grandfather donated those items willingly. He wanted everyone to share in their history."

I watch as emotions play across the man's face—grief, rage, desperation. My own voice surprises me as I step forward. "We can prove it. There are records, and documents in the archive. We can show you the truth about your grandfather's legacy."

But something in his expression shifts to a cornered look that makes my stomach drop. Before any of us can react, he turns and bolts toward the back of the house.

"After him!" Drew shouts, and we're running, our footsteps echoing off the brick walls.

The chase sends adrenaline surging through my veins. Clara splits off down a side alley while Drew and I pursue him directly. Mrs. Chen and Mr. Morrison take a different route, attempting to cut him off.

As we run, memories flash through my mind—cataloging artifacts on my first day, sharing laughs with Clara and Drew, discovering clues that led us here. Each moment has built to this, transforming me from an uncertain intern into someone who fights for what matters.

The man disappears around the corner of the house's storage entrance. Drew and I follow, our breath coming in sharp gasps. Inside, we find him frantically pulling at a large wooden box hidden behind some crates.

"Stop!" I command, surprising myself with the authority in my voice. "You're only making things worse."

Clara appears from another door, blocking his escape route. Mrs. Chen and Mr. Morrison aren't far behind. We've got him surrounded, the box of stolen artifacts within reach.

"Please," the man begs, his hands trembling on the box. "You don't know what it's like to lose your family's legacy."

I take a careful step forward. "But we do know. We've spent weeks understanding these artifacts, the stories they tell, the families they represent. Including yours. Your grandfather's story deserves to be told—but not like this."

Through the dim light of the storage room, I watch the man's shoulders slump in defeat. His trembling hands release the wooden box, and for the first time, I see beyond his anger to the pain beneath.

"Your name," I say softly. "Tell us who you are."

"Marcus Reynolds," he replies, his voice thick with emotion. "My grandfather's collection was his life's work. I grew up hearing stories about how this museum betrayed him, took everything he loved."

Drew steps forward, his expression thoughtful. "But that's not what really happened, is it? Mrs. Chen—she was there."

Clara moves closer to the box, her artist's eyes scanning the artifacts inside. "These pieces," she muses, "they're all connected to your grandfather's original donation. The missing heirlooms, the items from local homes—they're part of the same collection."

The pieces suddenly click in my mind. "You were trying to recreate his collection," I realize. "But why steal them? Why not just ask the museum?"

Marcus sinks onto a nearby crate, looking utterly exhausted. "I found his old journals in our attic last month. They detailed every piece, every story. But when I came to the museum to see them, some were in storage, others had been lent out to other institutions. It felt like his legacy was being dismantled."

Mrs. Chen approaches him with surprising gentleness. "Thomas was my friend, Marcus. He donated these items because he believed history belongs to everyone. He wanted to share these stories, not hoard them."

Drawing from my pocket, I pull out the photograph we found earlier. "Look," I say, showing him the image of his grandfather standing proudly in front of the museum's original display. "He's smiling. This was his dream—to create a place where everyone could experience these treasures."

Clara's face lights up with inspiration. "What if we created a special exhibit? We could showcase your grandfather's original collection, tell his story alongside the artifacts."

"We could include his journal entries," Drew adds enthusiastically. "Let people see the pieces through his eyes."

I watch as hope slowly replaces the desperation in Marcus's face. "You'd do that? Create an exhibit about him?"

"Not just about him," I say firmly. "About all the families who've contributed to this museum. About how these artifacts connect us all."

Tears well in Marcus's eyes as he reaches into the box, gently touching a tarnished pocket watch. "This was his favorite piece. He used to let me hold it when I was little, told me stories about how it crossed the ocean with our ancestors."

Mrs. Chen smiles warmly. "I remember. He would wind it every morning before opening the museum."

Working together, we carefully catalog each recovered item. As we do, Marcus shares the stories his grandfather told him, adding rich new layers to our understanding of each piece. Drew documents everything with his phone while Clara sketches quick impressions, capturing details we might have missed.

* * *

The next few hours pass in a blur of activity. We contact Ms. Martinez, who arrives quickly with a mixture of relief and understanding. Rather than pressing charges, she listens to our proposal about the new exhibit and enthusiastically agrees.

"This is exactly what the **Museum of Oddities** is about," she declares. "Not just preserving history, but bringing it to life through the stories we share."

A sharp click of heels against the storage room floor makes us all turn. Out of the shadows steps a tall woman with cropped silver hair and keen eyes, moving to stand beside Ms. Martinez. My heart skips a beat as I recognize her—I've seen her around the museum these past weeks, always in the background, always watching ... and, at the Chen Victorian ancestral home! *Lizabeth?!*

"Well done, Mei," she says, her voice carrying a hint of amusement. "I must say, you've impressed me with your detective work."

"Who are you?" I ask, stepping slightly closer to Drew and Clara.

"Lizabeth Moore," she replies, extending her hand. "Private investigator, hired by the museum after the first few disappearances. I've been tracking this case alongside you—though you might not have noticed me."

Heat rushes to my cheeks as I recall all the times I thought I glimpsed someone watching us. "You were following us?"

"Observing," Lizabeth corrects with a small smile. "When items first started vanishing, the museum brought me in to investigate. But then I noticed something interesting—a young intern who seemed to have natural detective instincts."

Drew nudges my shoulder. "See? I told you you were good at this."

"The way you connected the dots between the historical records and current events was particularly impressive," Lizabeth continues. "Most people would have missed the pattern with the emotional significance of each item."

Clara beams proudly. "Mei's always been good at understanding the stories behind things. It's like she can see connections others miss."

I feel a mixture of embarrassment and pride warming my chest. "I just... I wanted to understand why these specific items were being taken. It seemed important."

"It was," Lizabeth affirms. "And your approach—building trust, gathering information, working to understand motivations rather than just catching a culprit—that's what real detective work is about."

Ms. Martinez steps forward, her eyes twinkling. "That's exactly why I asked Lizabeth to keep an eye on you three. I had a feeling you might uncover more than just missing artifacts."

Marcus looks between us, still holding his grandfather's pocket watch. "So you knew? About me?"

"We suspected someone with inside knowledge was involved," Lizabeth explains. "But watching Mei and her friends piece together the family connections helped us understand the whole story. Sometimes the best way to solve a mystery is to let it unfold naturally."

"But you could have stopped me at any time," Marcus says, his voice thick with emotion.

"We could have," Lizabeth agrees. "But then we might have missed the chance to heal old wounds and set things right."

I look around at the recovered artifacts, thinking about all we've learned. "Each piece tells a story, doesn't it? Not just about the past, but about the people who've cared for them, who've passed them down."

"Precisely," Lizabeth says, fixing me with an appraising look. "You know, there's a summer program for young detectives at the city museum. Based on what I've seen, you'd be an excellent candidate."

My eyes widen. "Really?"

"The deadline for applications is next week," she continues, pulling a business card from her jacket pocket. "If you're interested, I'd be happy to recommend you."

Drew grabs my arm excitedly. "Mei, that's perfect for you!"

Clara nods enthusiastically. "You have to apply! Just think of all the mysteries you could solve!"

I take the card with slightly trembling fingers, remembering how uncertain I felt at the beginning of this internship. Now, standing here among friends old and new, surrounded by recovered artifacts and solved mysteries, I realize how much I've grown.

Ms. Martinez claps her hands together. "Well, we have quite a bit of work ahead of us. These artifacts need to be properly documented and stored, and we have a new exhibit to plan."

"I can help," Marcus offers quietly. "I know all my grandfather's stories about these pieces."

"And I can create illustrations for the display," Clara chimes in. "Really bring the history to life."

Drew pulls out his phone. "I've got photos of everything we've discovered. Plus, I could help set up some interactive digital displays about the investigation itself."

. . .

Standing in the museum's main hall later that evening, I look around at my friends—at Clara adding final touches to her sketches, at Drew arranging the recovered artifacts in their temporary display, at Mrs. Chen, Mr. Morrison, and Marcus deep in conversation about his grandfather's legacy. My heart swells with pride and affection.

"We did it," I whisper to myself, hardly believing how far we've come from that first day of my internship.

"Yes, we did," Drew says, appearing beside me with a grin. "Not bad for a bunch of interns, huh?"

Clara joins us, her sketchbook hugged to her chest. "Just wait until you see my designs for the exhibit. It's going to be amazing."

Looking at them both, I feel decades of history settling into place around us, old wounds healing through new understanding. Marcus's story isn't just about lost artifacts—it's about finding connections, about understanding that our histories are intertwined in ways we never imagined.

THE END

You Might Also Like

JOURNEY TO CRYSTAL LAKE
PART ONE

ESCAPE THE ORDINARY. FIND YOUR SPARK.

Get swept away with Journey to Crystal Lake, a thrilling YA romance in two parts!

Maddie's annual camping trip takes a dramatic turn when a blizzard tears through the mountains, separating her from her family. Lost and alone, she finds herself in a deserted cabin... with Dex, the infuriatingly handsome boy from school who secretly holds her heart.

Will they find their way back together, or will the storm ignite a bitterness even fiercer than the blizzard?

Part One!

Young Adult Romance

by Lia Lucas

Ebook & Paperback

SNOWBOUND WITH THE BOY NEXT DOOR
PART TWO

ADVENTURE AWAITS...

Maddie's annual camping trip takes a dramatic turn when a blizzard tears through the mountains, separating her from her family. Seeking refuge in a deserted cabin, she encounters the last person she expects – Dex, the infuriatingly handsome boy from high school and the campsite next door.

Sparks fly in the face of danger...

Forced to rely on each other for survival, Maddie and Dex's

contrasting personalities clash at first. But as the storm rages on, shared stories and flickering candlelight ignite an unexpected warmth between them.

Will their love weather the storm?

With dwindling supplies and no way to contact help, their newfound connection faces its ultimate test. Can their bond survive the harsh reality of their situation, or will it melt away like the snow?

Discover a captivating story of resilience, adventure, and unexpected love.

Part Two!

Young Adult Romance

by Lia Lucas

Ebook & Paperback

STAR-CROSSED RIVALS

OPPOSITES ATTRACT. OR REPEL.

Avery's the golden child.

Noah's the rebel with a cause. They hate each other. But when forced to partner for the school's Shakespeare competition, their world collides.

Will sparks fly, or will their rivalry consume them?

Dive into a captivating tale of love, hate, and everything in between.

> Opposites attract...or do they? Find out in this sizzling YA romance.
>
> Ebook & Paperback

Haunted Hearts

A SUMMER CAMP. A TRAGIC PAST. A GHOST WITH AN UNFULFILLED LONGING.

Can you feel a chill?

Riley thought summer camp would be filled with friends, campfires, and maybe a little flirting. But when she arrives at the rumored haunted camp, she discovers a secret world beyond her wildest imagination. There, she encounters the ghost of a dashing young counselor, trapped between the living and the dead.

As their connection deepens, Riley must navigate the complexities of a forbidden love while unraveling the chilling mystery surrounding the ghost's tragic demise. Will their love story be a haunting memory or a chance for redemption?

Prepare to be captivated by a tale of love, loss, and the supernatural.

Young Adult Romance

Ebook & Paperback

THE SECRET RECIPE SOCIETY

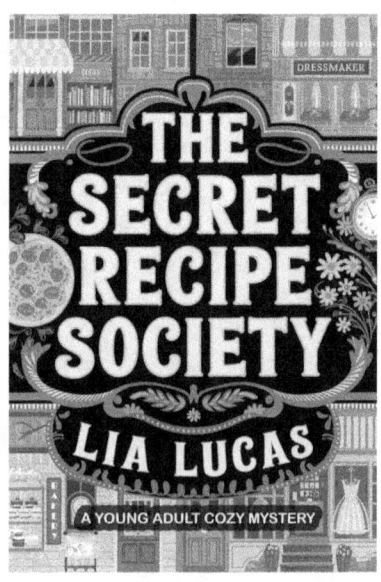

UNLEASH YOUR INNER DETECTIVE! ARE YOU READY TO CRACK THE CODE?

When 16-year-old Sophie inherits her grandmother's beloved bakery, she uncovers more than just delicious recipes. Hidden within an ancient cookbook lies a secret society, a group of town protectors who used their storefronts to solve mysteries and keep their community safe.

But danger lurks in the shadows. Local businesses are

receiving chilling threats, and Sophie fears her grandmother's bakery could be next. With the help of Jason, whose family runs the local bookshop, Sophie must decipher her grandmother's cryptic clues and unravel the truth before it's too late.

"The Secret Recipe Society" is a thrilling YA mystery that will keep you guessing until the very last page.

Available in

Ebook & Paperback

THE MIDNIGHT GARDEN CLUB

UNCOVER THE SECRETS OF THE MIDNIGHT GARDEN CLUB! CAN LUCY SOLVE THE MYSTERY BEFORE IT'S TOO LATE?

When aspiring botanist Lucy moves in with her aunt for senior year, she's eager to join the school's gardening club. But she soon discovers it's no ordinary club – it's a secret society of student detectives who solve campus mysteries under the cover of night!

When rare plants begin disappearing from the school greenhouse, including a newly discovered species named after the retiring principal, Lucy is determined to use her botanical knowledge and the club's investigative skills to track down the culprit.

However, as the clues unfold, Lucy begins to suspect a darker connection: the thefts may be linked to her late mother's own mysterious past at the very same school.

"The Midnight Garden Club" is a thrilling YA mystery that blends botanical intrigue with a touch of supernatural suspense.

Available in

Ebook & Paperback

About Lia

Lia Lucas is an emerging author of Urban Fiction, Young Adult, and Contemporary Romance. She has a wide range of writing interests and is currently living an incognito digital lifestyle.

Ms. Lucas is part of the Ardent Artist Books family.

Lia has published several books.

- youtube.com/theardentartist
- amazon.com/stores/Ardent-Artist-Books/author/B08BX8F1DZ

Also by Lia

YOUNG ♦ ADULT

Journey To Crystal Lake - Part One

Snowbound with the Boy Next Door - Part Two

Star-Crossed Rivals

* * *

YOUNG ♦ ADULT ♦ SERIES

The Haunted Hearts Series

Haunted Hearts - Book 1

Ink and Ashes - Book 2

Ghosts in the Attic - Book 3

* * *

Standalone YA Cozy Mysteries

Museum of Lost Things

The Secret Recipe Society

The Midnight Garden Club

* * *

18+ ♦ Adult

Curves

She Was Going Home

www.ingramcontent.com/pod-product-compliance
Lightning Source LLC
LaVergne TN
LVHW021826060526
838201LV00058B/3519